W·D...

D0852285

Who's Going to Take Care of Me?

Who's Going to Take Care of Me?

by Michelle Magorian

Pictures by James Graham Hale

Harper & Row, Publishers

Library of Congress Cataloging-in-Publication Data
Magorian, Michelle.
    Who's going to take care of me? / Michelle Magorian ; pictures by
James Graham Hale.
        p.   cm.
    Summary: Having attended daycare with his sister, Eric wonders
who will look after him there, now that his sister is old enough to go
to school.
    ISBN 0-06-024105-5 : $ · — ISBN 0-06-024106-3 (lib. bdg.) :
$
    [1. Day care centers—Fiction.   2. Brothers and sisters—Fiction.]
I. Hale, James Graham, ill.   II. Title
PZ7.M275Wh   1990   89-26741
[E]—dc20   CIP
                                                                  AC

For Charlotte Zolotow

Eric and Karin were brother and sister.
Before the summer, they went to day care together.

Karin was older than Eric.
She showed him where the big wax crayons were
and brought him large pieces of paper.

She took him to the sandbox and helped him
build castles.

After the summer, Karin wasn't going to day care anymore.
She was going to school.

Mom bought Karin new shoes for school.
But she didn't buy any for Eric.

Dad gave Karin a pencil case for school.
But he didn't give one to Eric.

And they talked about school with Karin
in the kitchen

in the garden

and at bedtime.

Eric just listened.
He felt small.

"Who's going to take care of me," he thought, "when Karin goes to school?
Who will teach me the words to the songs?
Who will I sit with at story time?"

One morning, Karin put on her new blouse
      her new skirt
      her new sweater
      her new socks
    and her new shoes.
"I'm going to school," she said, and ran downstairs.

Eric got dressed by himself.
It took a long time.
"Hurry up," his mother called up the stairs,
"or Karin will be late."

When Eric came downstairs, Karin laughed.
"Your shirt buttons aren't in the right holes," she said.
"And your sweater's inside out.
Look—your shoes are on the wrong feet."

"It doesn't matter, Eric," said his mother.
"You've done very well."
She helped him put his clothes right.
But Eric felt small.

Outside the school gates, Eric and his mother waved good-bye to Karin. They watched her walk into school with all the other children.
A lot of them were taller and older than Karin.
"That's funny," said Eric.
"Karin looks small."

Eric and his mother arrived at day care.
Two of his friends ran up to him.
"Hello, Eric," they cried.
"Hello, Hildie," he said. "Hello, Robert."

And they played.

Later, when they were having a rest and
drinking their juice, Eric noticed a little boy
sitting by himself in a corner.
It was his first time at day care.
He looked scared.

Eric went over to him.
"Come with me," he said.

He showed him where the big wax crayons were
and brought him large pieces of paper.

He took him to the sandbox and helped him build castles.
And he taught him the words to the songs.

When it was story time, the little boy asked,
"Can I sit next to you?"
"Sure," said Eric.
The little boy smiled.

Eric put his arm around his shoulders and grinned back.
Suddenly, he didn't feel small anymore.
He felt big.